First published 2020 by Nosy Crow Ltd
The Crow's Nest, 14 Baden Place, Crosby Row,
London SE1 1YW
www.nosycrow.com

ISBN 978 1 78800 446 6

A CIP catalogue record for this book is available
from the British Library.

Printed in China

MIX
Paper from
responsible sources
FSC® C104723

Papers used by Nosy Crow are made from wood
grown in sustainable forests.

10 9 8 7 6

For Quinn, with love
from Auntie Jeannie xx
– JW

For Emily,
my wonderful little girl
– IF

JEANNE WILLIS AND ISABELLE FOLLATH

WHat ARE Little GiRLS MADE oF?

To Mhairi
Happy 2nd Birthday!
Lots of love, your pal
Peigi xxx ♡♡

nosy crow

WHAT ARE LITTLE GIRLS MADE OF?

What are little girls made of?
What are little girls made of?
Sun and rain and heart and brain —
that's what girls are made of.

What are little boys made of?
What are little boys made of?
Except for little things, much the same —
that's what boys are made of.

GEORGIE PORGIE

Georgie Porgie, pudding and pie,
kissed a girl who made him cry.
"Don't kiss me unless I say!"
she said, and kicked his ball away.

LITTLE JADE HORNER

Little Jade Horner
sat in a corner,
staring up at the stars.
She made little spaceships
from saucepans and hair clips,
and sent all her teddies to Mars.

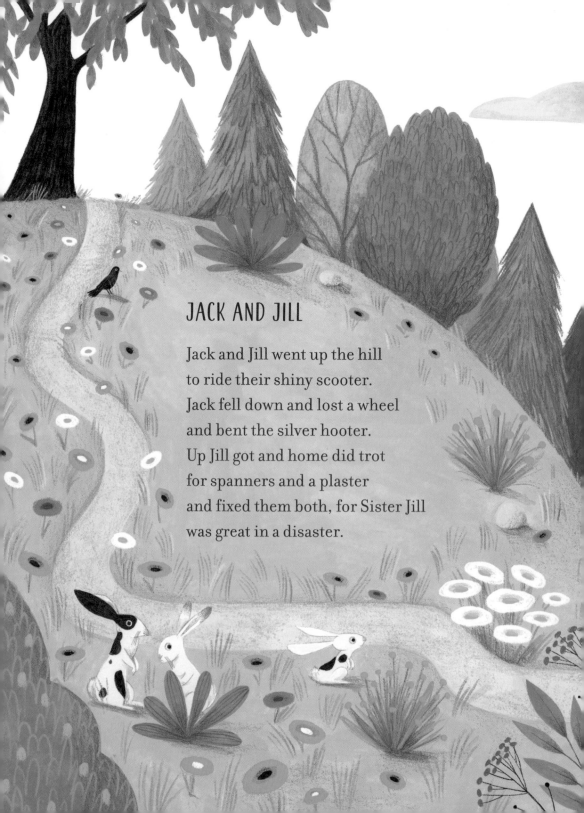

JACK AND JILL

Jack and Jill went up the hill
to ride their shiny scooter.
Jack fell down and lost a wheel
and bent the silver hooter.
Up Jill got and home did trot
for spanners and a plaster
and fixed them both, for Sister Jill
was great in a disaster.

BYE, BABY BUNTING

Bye, Baby Bunting,
Mummy's gone job-hunting
to pay for university
so you can get a good degree.

LITTLE MISS MUFFET

Little Miss Muffet
sat on a tuffet
eating her ham and eggs,
and when a big spider
then sat down beside her,
she stroked his sweet, long, furry legs.

INCY WINCY SPIDER

Incy Wincy Spider, climbing up the spout,
in came Lorraine and helped the spider out.
She put him in the garden to catch the pesky flies
and all the flowers that she grew won first prize.

LAVENDER'S BLUE

Lavender's blue, dilly dilly,
lavender's green,
you shan't be king, silly billy,
I shall be queen!

DOCTOR FOSTER

Doctor Foster went to Gloucester
in a shower of rain.
She fell in a puddle right up to her middle,
and fixed the broken drain.

WHERE ARE YOU GOING TO, MY PRETTY MAID?

"Where are you going to, my pretty maid?"
"Off to school, of course," she said.
"May I go with you, my pretty maid?"
"You can if you want to, boy," she said.
"What does your mummy do, my pretty maid?"
"She is a surgeon, boy," she said.
"What is your fortune, my pretty maid?"
"My brains are my fortune, boy," she said.
"Then I can't marry you, my pretty maid."
"Boy, I am glad of that," she said.

BONNIE SHAFTO

Bonnie Shafto's gone to sea,
silver cutlass on her knee,
fighting pirates, one, two, three,
ahoy there, Bonnie Shafto!

Bonnie Shafto's brave and bold,
though the waves are icy cold,
and she's only six years old,
yo-ho, Bonnie Shafto!

DIDDLE DIDDLE DUMPLING

Diddle diddle dumpling, Brother John
went to bed with his night light on,
afraid in case a monster came,
which really was a crying shame.
Diddle diddle dumpling, Sister Jane
turned his night light off again.
"There are no monsters, it is true,"
she said, "except for me and you!"

HUMPTY DUMPTY

Humpty Dumpty sat on a wall,
Humpty Dumpty had a great fall.
The doctor arrived
and she mended his shell
and dried all his eggy tears
gently as well.

TWINKLE, TWINKLE

"Twinkle, twinkle, Little Star.
How I wonder what you are?"
"I have often wondered too,"
 said the star, "now, who are you?"

So I answered, "I am me!"
and the star said, "Ah, I see!
I'm no longer in the dark,
as you're by far the brightest spark."

MARY, MARY

Mary, Mary, quite contrary,
always changing her style –
so sometimes she's a fairy queen
and other times, she's a crocodile!

LITTLE BO-PEEP

Little Bo-Peep had lost her sheep,
they fell in a ditch full of slime.
She waded straight in, right up to her chin,
and rescued them one at a time.

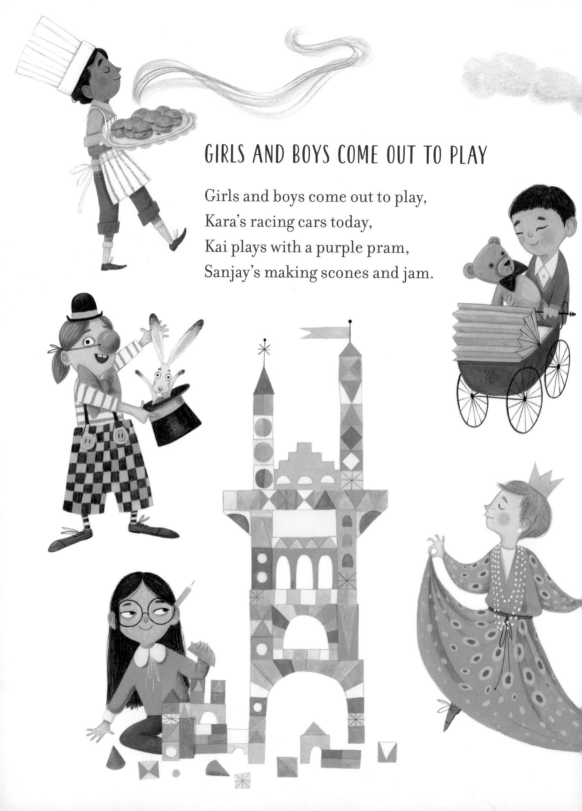

GIRLS AND BOYS COME OUT TO PLAY

Girls and boys come out to play,
Kara's racing cars today,
Kai plays with a purple pram,
Sanjay's making scones and jam.

Belle has built a bridge with bricks,
Kate's performing circus tricks,
Joe is wearing fancy dress –
he's a beautiful princess.

Phil and Fay pretend to fight,
(Phil's a dragon, Fay's a knight),
Ray is dancing a ballet –
we play what we want to play!